LEGENDS
ANTHONY HOROWITZ
Tricks and Transformations

Illustrated by Thomas Yeates

KINGFISHER

NEW YORK

Distributed in the U.S. and Canada by Macmillan, 175 Fifth Ave., New
York, NY 10010

Library of Congress Cataloging-in-Publication data
has been applied for.

ISBN 978-0-7534-6545-5

Kingfisher books are available for special promotions and premiums.
For more details contact: Special Markets Department, Macmillan, 175
Fifth Ave., New York, NY 10010

For more information, please visit
www.kingfisherbooks.com

Printed and bound by CPI Group (U.K.) Ltd., Croydon CR0 4YY
1 3 5 7 9 8 6 4 2

Contents

Introduction

Because Kingfisher has released these myths and legends in six colorful and delightfully illustrated volumes, this is the sixth introduction that I've had to write. It is also the last. So maybe it's the right time to consider what this has all been about.

It occurred to me, rereading the Japanese myth of the first eclipse and even the Greek myth of Pan and Syrinx—both of which appear in this volume and both of which are "origin" stories in that they try to explain how things began—that it's a shame we don't have myths and legends anymore. These old stories may have been improbable and even ridiculous, but they added a color and a gaiety to life that is sadly lacking today. Take a look at the sky. Does it delight you to know that a solar eclipse is an astronomical event that occurs when Earth intersects the umbra portion of the Moon's shadow and that it can last up to seven minutes and thirty one seconds? Or would you prefer to imagine that it is the result of a vain and foolish goddess being trapped inside a cave by a beautiful woman who turns out to be her own reflection?

As I've mentioned elsewhere, many of the stars and planets are named after characters who first appeared in ancient mythology. Mars was the god of war, Venus the goddess of love etcetera. But nowadays we have forgotten their stories and tend to think of them only in terms of mass, distance, hydrostatic equilibrium, and so on. You may not have heard of this last expression, but it's apparently the reason why planets are spherical. Personally I'd have been happier if someone had told me that Zeus had used them to make doughballs or had needed them to play marbles with Poseidon.

The trouble is that we live in a world where everything has an explanation. When even the human DNA, the very stuff we're made of, has been unraveled, how can there be mysteries anymore? There used to be a time when we were afraid of nature, but now we believe that we have the upper hand, and it's only on those rare occasions that disasters happen—tsunamis and earthquakes—that we are reminded who is truly in command. And we are a metropolitan age. The chances are that you are reading this in a town or a city. Almost certainly you are in a comfortable house, behind double glazing, cut off from nature. You no longer have any reason to be afraid.

This is a pity. I spend a lot of time in Orford, in Suffolk, England, and one of the reasons I like it so much is that it's infused with stories. Rendlesham Forest, nearby, is the location of one of the most notorious UFO sightings (it happened in December 1980—check it out on the Internet). It's also the site of a top secret U.S. airbase, where some say the stealth bomber was first put through its paces. Pirates and smugglers were active all along the coast hundreds of years ago, while an entire village mysteriously disappeared beneath the sea at nearby Dunwich. A mermaid or some similar sea creature was once spotted in the River Alde. The atomic bomb that fell on Hiroshima was tested on Orford Ness—just opposite my house— and radar (which began its life as a would-be death ray to knock out German planes) was invented a few miles along the coast. There's even a story, almost certainly untrue, that the famous bouncing bomb was developed nearby and accidentally blew up a pub.

When I walk in Suffolk, with the huge skies, the wind sweeping in all the way from Russia and the sea a shimmering, metallic gray, I think about these stories and it seems to me that where we live and the stories we tell are in some way vital to each other. They are interconnected. They need each other to be fully alive.

So it's a shame that very few mysteries have survived to the modern age. Many people still believe in UFOs, while others are happy to chase after the Loch Ness monster or the Abominable Snowman. For a brief time crop circles excited us, because we weren't exactly sure how they were created, and we're still looking for places that may or may not have existed—such as El Dorado, the lost city of gold, and the ancient civilization of Atlantis. You might say that Jack the Ripper fascinates us, not because he was the first modern serial killer, but because we never found out who he was—he wasn't caught.

This is the curse of the time we live in. On the one hand, we crave mystery. It's part of human nature. On the other, we have to face up to cold reality. Almost everything has been explained.

Maybe one day I'll write a seventh volume of myths and legends, a collection of brand-new stories providing answers to the questions that science hasn't fully disentangled. Why do we yawn? Why do we blush when we tell a lie? How did the first kiss happen? How do birds flying south form such wonderful patterns in the sky? What actually happens when we go to sleep? If a cow sits down, does it really mean it's going to rain? Why do we have hair on some parts of our bodies but not on others? (We're very similar to apes, but in this one respect we're their complete opposite. No scientist—bald or otherwise—has come up with a full explanation.)

But until then, this is the last collection in the series and I hope you enjoy it. Even reading these stories helps to keep them alive—and that's got to be worth something in itself.

Anthony Horowitz

The Hounds of Actaeon

Greek

The Hounds of Actaeon

It had been a long day and the sun was sinking wearily behind the mountains of Orchomenus. But if the sky was the color of blood, it found a cruel reflection in the valleys and fields. For Actaeon had been at work. Actaeon the son of Aristaeus who invented the art of beekeeping. Actaeon the most famous huntsman in ancient Greece.

When the horn of Actaeon was heard echoing through the forests, then the animals would tremble and the birds would rise,

crashing through the undergrowth. From first light to last, he and his friends would spread their bloody net over the countryside and nothing would escape them; not the meanest fox, nor the fastest deer. And every night the fire in his banqueting hall would crackle as the fat from fresh venison dripped into the flames and the smell of the roasting meat would reach the lonely shepherds on their slopes twenty miles away.

Actaeon's cloak was lined with fur, and his palace walls with the heads of his catches. There was not an inch of the place that was not covered with some kind of animal pelt, and even his chairs were fashioned from antlers. But it was not for these ornaments nor for the taste of meat that Actaeon delighted to hunt. It was for the love of the hunt itself: the scent, the pursuit, the trap, the kill. The fall, when the leaves were turning and some of the heat had gone out of the sun, that was his favorite time of year. Then he would invite his friends out with him into the fields, urging them forward with all the eagerness of a general rallying his troops for war.

Not one, not two, but fifty hunting dogs went with him, and every single one of them was dear to him. He treated them like children (for he had no children of his own), feeding them with his own hand at the dinner table and making sure that they were all comfortably kenneled at night before going to bed himself. Each dog had a name and a character and each dog knew its exact place in the hunt.

There was Pterelas, the fastest of the pack. Once an animal was spotted, he would race forward to head it off. There was Theron, the fearless. He would hurl himself past raking claw or kicking foot to lunge at the quarry's throat. Old Ichnobates was respected for his wisdom. Should the pack come across a false scent in the wood, he would know which direction to follow. No dog was more savage than Nape. His mother had been a

wolf and he took as much pleasure in the hunt as Actaeon himself. Then there was Nebrophonus the strong, Melampus the Spartan, Harpalus the spotted, Lachne the shaggy . . . fifty dogs, each with its own talents to add to the kill.

It was the end of another fall day and Actaeon was counting the number of animals that he and his pack had slaughtered. The dogs were tired, their coats matted with blood and sweat, but their tails were high and their eyes excited. For they had done their work well. Thirty carcasses lay heaped up on the grass, blood flowing sluggishly from gaping wounds and flies buzzing round sightless eyes. Now the dogs looked forward to a well-deserved rest and to a supper of rib bone for each one of them. Actaeon's friends, too, would be glad to get back to the palace. First they would bathe; then rest. And when the moon was out and the stars were shining, the wine flowing and the minstrels playing, there would be a great feast, a chance to swap adventures, and to tell once again all the old hunting tales.

Actaeon stepped forward and raised a hand for silence. He was a young man, in his early thirties, with fair hair and dark brown eyes—not that you could have told as much from looking at him for he was drenched in blood from head to foot.

"My friends," he said. "We have hunted enough for one day. Let us fold up our nets and put away our weapons. Tomorrow, at dawn, we can return to the fields and, who knows, perhaps we'll even manage to beat today's tally. Thirty dead, my friends. Thirty more trophies for my palace walls. A successful hunt indeed!"

The guests began to make their way home, but Actaeon, still intoxicated by the scent of blood, decided to walk a little in the evening air. He therefore climbed back down the hill and across a valley where pine trees and cypresses were growing in thick clusters. After only a few minutes he found himself completely alone. Everything was silent. There wasn't so much as a rustle in the undergrowth.

"We have killed every animal in the valley," Actaeon muttered to himself with a vague smile. "Or if there are any survivors they are too afraid to move."

But then he frowned because he could hear something. Where was it coming from? He listened carefully. Years of hunting had developed his hearing to the extent that the sound of a twig breaking one hundred yards away would not escape him. And there could be no mistaking the sound he was hearing now. It was just that it was so unexpected, so out-of-place. It was the sound of women laughing.

He tiptoed through a clump of trees, again using his skills as a huntsman to ensure that he made absolutely no noise. Now the laughter was louder, nearer, and he could also hear splashing. There was a slight rise in the ground and he got on to his hands and knees, snaking through the dust and pine needles.

". . . and the scorpion stung him on the heel and that was the end of that."

Actaeon heard the woman's voice before he saw her. She had just finished telling a story and the other women—there must have been about a dozen of them—laughed. At last he reached the top of the hillock. Slowly, he lifted his head and gazed in astonishment.

There was a clearing in the wood in the center of which was a pool of limpid water, fed by a spring that gushed out of a nearby rock face, curtaining down over the entrance to a cave. The cave had been carved by hand rather than by nature for it was ornamented with stone pillars and garlands. The pool was surrounded by a carpet of grass and moss. Bloated flowers hanging heavy on slender stalks sprouted everywhere and the smell of perfume was overpowering. The sun was now almost beneath the horizon, but pink and silver shafts of light slanted down into the secret grotto from a perfect full moon.

No fewer than twenty young girls surrounded the pool, some sitting on the bank with their legs in the water, some kneeling among the flowers. One woman stood in their midst, completely naked, her hands cupped to pour water as she washed herself. She was the woman who had spoken and Actaeon knew who she was even before he saw her quiver and arrows lying on the grass.

The girls were nymphs. The woman was the goddess Artemis.

Artemis was the goddess of the moon which even now hung like a vast paper lantern in the sky above her. She was also the goddess of hunting and many times had Actaeon sacrificed to her after a successful day. But far from being pleased to see him, he realized with a surge of fear that if she discovered him there he was doomed. For Artemis was renowned for her chastity. It was well known that she had actually put one of her nymphs—Callisto—to death for daring to be seduced by Zeus. Her followers lived under the strictest moral code. And for her to be spied on, in her nakedness, by a mere mortal . . . well, it was unthinkable.

But fearful though he was, he could not tear his eyes away from the scene. The goddess, after all, personified everything he held most dear. Moreover, she was beautiful. Startlingly beautiful.

She was tall and strong, with narrow hips and long, straight limbs. And yet her flesh looked soft and inviting. Her hair, the color of leaves in the fall, fell almost to her knees in golden streams. At moments her face was a little severe, but when she laughed (and while she continued telling her story about the divine hunter, Orion, she laughed often) she had the most beautiful smile. She looked gentle and kind; and Actaeon was certain that no man had ever seen her like this before. He dared not stay. But he could not leave.

Why Artemis spotted him, nobody knows. Perhaps he made a noise or perhaps, being a huntress herself and an immortal as well, his very breathing was enough to give him away. But suddenly her face froze and her eyes widened in shock and outrage. The nymphs screamed and scrabbled for her clothes while her hands crossed and clasped her shoulders, hiding herself. Feeling the blood rush to his cheeks, Actaeon stood up, trying to find the words to apologize for his intrusion. No words came. The eyes of the goddess were on him now and it was as if they were splitting his head in two. He groaned in pain, clutching his skull in his hands. There was a loud cracking sound and something sprouted out of his hair. With a strangled cry, he reeled backward, tripping and rolling over on the ground.

He tried to get up, then jerked violently as his back was seized by a sudden terrible convulsion. He felt his spine bending— snapping. Somehow his clothes had been torn from him and his whole body seemed to be covered in pine needles or . . . was it fur? He opened his mouth and was horrified to see an enormous tongue loll over his chin, a tongue that could not possibly belong to him. He was on all fours now. It was the only position that seemed comfortable. And then it was over as suddenly as it had begun. His

pulse slowed down. He breathed normally. The pain had gone.

But what had happened to him? Still on all fours he climbed the hillock and walked—or was he crawling?—over to the pool. Artemis and her retinue had gone, the grotto was empty, but he could still distinguish their scent beneath the heavier smell of the flowers—and that too was strange for although his senses had always been sharp, surely they had never been that sharp. He looked down into the water. Then he understood.

A reflection of a stag looked back at him. For that was what he was. That was what he had become. He tried to scratch his head but found that his front leg would not reach. Artemis had turned him into a stag! It was monstrous . . . monstrously unfair. It hadn't been his fault that he had seen her bathing. She hadn't even given him a chance to apologize or explain.

He stood there for a long time, wondering

what he was going to do. All in all it was rather a dilemma. He didn't know how long the goddess intended him to remain a stag and back at the palace his guests would be waiting for him, wondering what had happened. Should he go back? No. What would they say when a stag walked in and took his place at the head of the table?

And then he heard something that sent a wave of sheer terror crashing through him. It was a sound to freeze his blood and turn every muscle in his body to water.

It was the sound of barking.

For his fifty dogs, having waited patiently for their master to return, had come in search of him. And they had picked up a new scent in the air. The scent of a stag. The hounds of Actaeon were coming. They were coming now.

He was too frightened to think. Instead he trusted to instinct . . . the instinct of a stag. He turned, tried to run. But his legs were twisted. One caught against another and he almost tripped. He opened his mouth to shout the command that would send the pack in another direction, but no sound came out. Then he was running, breaking through the undergrowth, feeling the rhythm beneath him, faster and faster.

For the first and the last time in his life he experienced the "thrill" of the hunt from the quarry's point of view. He could not see the dogs, dared not stop to see if they were catching up. He could hear nothing above the sound of his own tortured breathing. All he could do was run, uncaring where he went. Faster! In his blind panic he smashed into a tree. The branches tore at his face. Now he could taste blood. He had bitten through his tongue. Faster! He had glimpsed a dark shape out of the corner of his eye. It was a dog. They were catching up with him. Faster! His heart was going to burst. Surely

they would tire soon, forget him, leave him alone. He couldn't go much further. He was seeing the forest through a pulsating red film. Tears of uncontrollable terror were pouring from his eyes. His whole body was drenched in sweat.

Faster! Faster! Faster!

But still they came, the hounds of Actaeon. Pterelas, racing ahead to cut him off. Theron, homing in on his throat. Ichnobates keeping the pack on his trail. Nape, bringing the cruelty and ferocity of a wolf to the pursuit . . .

The light of the moon was relentless. The trees stood black and rigid, like iron bars. The forest seemed to stretch on forever. And the dogs ran, their teeth bared, their eyes aglow. They would not stop. They would never stop. Not until they had killed.

That was how they had been trained.

The First Eclipse

Japanese

The First Eclipse

There have been good gods and there have been bad gods, but there have been few gods as difficult and as generally objectionable as Susanoo, the Japanese god of the sea, of thunder, rain and wind, and of fertility. Perhaps his early years were partly to blame. It cannot be very easy growing up in the knowledge that you started life in your father's nose. But then his sister, Amaterasu, sprang to life at the same moment from her father's left eye and she was as divine as only a goddess of the sun can be.

But to begin at the beginning . . .

The father of Susanoo and Amaterasu was called Izanagi. He was one of the first of the Japanese gods and the father of virtually all of the gods that followed—as well as of the eight principal islands of Japan. His marriage came to a tragic end, however, when his wife, whose name was Izanami, was burned to death while giving birth to the god of fire. Izanagi wept bitterly at her loss and more gods sprang from his every tear.

In his anger, he cut the head off the god of fire and yet more gods were born in the splashing of blood. All this goes some way toward explaining why there are so many gods in Japan.

Meanwhile, Izanami had gone down to the Underworld and Izanagi decided to bring her back.

"Am I not a god?" he said to himself. "Am I not the father of all the gods? Why should she be taken from me? Izanami is beautiful. Her skin is so fair, her hair so dark, her eyes so like the color of emeralds. I will not live without her! She shall come back to me."

And with these words he hurried down to the Underworld and banged on the door of the house in which she was living.

"Izanami!" he called out. "It is me. Izanagi. I have come to take you home."

"Leave me!" a voice cried from within. "I am not ready for you. Go and speak with the king of the Underworld. He will tell you when I can leave."

"Nobody tells me anything!" Izanagi shouted, growing angry. "I am the god of the gods and you will come with me."

"Not yet!"

"You will come this instant."

Now red with anger, Izanagi kicked down the door and walked into the house. But he had forgotten the destructive power of death. The sight that greeted him on the other side of the door was not his beautiful wife but a hideous spectacle, a rotting, decomposing corpse with worms where there should have been eyes, glistening bones where there should have been soft flesh. With a terrible scream he turned and ran. He did not stop running until he had left the Underworld and reached the sea. Without even stopping to take a breath, he dived in. At once the sound of his own screams was cut off, and his body turned slowly in a world of shimmering blue silence, his robes billowing around him and bubbles streaming from his nose and mouth. It was as if he needed the expanse of a whole ocean to cleanse the horror of what he had seen. And so it was. The icy water shattered the memory then washed away the fragments. When he climbed on to the shore, Izanami and her home in the Underworld were forgotten.

Susanoo and Amaterasu were born at the same moment beneath the ocean, carried away from their father's body in a whirlpool of bubbles. When at last they reached the surface, their father was already gone,

turning his back on them. And so it was that the god of the sea and the goddess of the sun were born.

Susanoo Goes Too Far

While Amaterasu quietly took her place in the heavens, providing the world with light and warmth, Susanoo—whose name can be translated to mean "swift, headstrong god"—took every opportunity to squabble with his father. At last the old god came to the end of his tether and after a particularly violent disagreement, banished his son to the

The First Eclipse

province of Izumo which is on the coast of the Sea of Japan.

Before he went, however, he decided to travel up to heaven in order to say goodbye to his sister, whom he had not seen since they were born. As usual he went with a great deal of noise and confusion, shaking the mountains and making the whole world tremble. Hearing him coming, Amaterasu grew alarmed. A stampede of elephants or an army on the warpath would have made less of a commotion. Certainly it was not the sound of a brother coming to visit. Afraid for her life, she reached for her bow and when Susanoo arrived, he found the point of an arrow aimed straight at his heart.

"Keep back!" Amaterasu warned.

"What's going on here?" Susanoo cried. "Our honorable father kicks me out of the heavens and now my beloved sister wants to pin me to a cloud!"

"Why have you come?"

"To say goodbye."

"Goodbye?" Still she aimed the arrow at her brother, the bowstring taut in her fingers. "Why should I believe you?"

"Because I'm your brother, for heaven's sake! Look—I'll tell you what. Let us, you and I, create eight more gods. They'll be a sort of token between us, proof that no matter what may happen now or in the future, we remain brother and sister, and friends. Our children will be the founders of the royal house of Japan and everyone will know that we were their parents. Our children! What do you say?"

Then Amaterasu's heart softened. She set down her bow and arrow and took instead her brother's sword which she broke into three pieces. These she placed in her mouth.

The First Eclipse

A moment later she blew out a silvery mist in which three young girls appeared. For his part, Susanoo reached for the five jewels that hung on his sister's necklace and broke them between his teeth. Five young gods leaped out of the pieces. Five boys and three girls: thus were the first ancestors of the Japanese created.

Amaterasu smiled to see what she had done. But as usual, Susanoo's excitement was so great as to be positively dangerous. First he ruined all the rice fields by filling in the irrigation ditches. Then he caused havoc in the sacred temple that had been built for the fruit festival. Finally he ran, laughing, up to his elderly horse and—rather in the manner of a conjuror whipping away a tablecloth without disturbing the cups and plates—pulled off the wretched animal's skin in one piece. The bloody corpse he hurled into the air and, still shrieking with laughter, hurried off to find something else to destroy.

The First Eclipse

All this was bad enough but what was even worse was that the horse landed on the roof of Amaterasu's house, smashing right through in a shower of tiles and straw. It finally came to rest in the sewing room.

Amaterasu was sewing at the time.

You can imagine how she felt. There she was, one minute putting a final stitch in the hem of a kimono. The next, the roof was collapsing all around her and a great lump of dead horse was splattering itself all over her sewing machine. In a second the whole room was a mass of screaming women. Two servants fainted. A third fell into her machine and managed to stitch a perfect line across her own throat before she succumbed. As for Amaterasu, she was so frightened

that she ran out of the house and hid herself in a dark cave, pulling an enormous boulder across the entrance so that no one could follow her in. At once the world was plunged into darkness.

And that, some scholars say, was the first eclipse.

The Rival

Susanoo received a severe punishment for his misbehavior. He had already been banished from heaven, but now his beard and mustache were cut off and all his fingernails and toenails were pulled out with tweezers. As a matter of fact, he became something of a reformed character after this, performing many great and heroic deeds in the province of Izumo.

But meanwhile, the other gods were faced with a problem. They had seen Amaterasu run into the cave so at least they knew where to find her. The question was, how could they entice her out and so end the darkness that had fallen on the world? One god suggested brute force, but that was soon rejected as Amaterasu would only hide again once they had gone. Another suggested bribing her with a nice juicy snake, but after her experience with the flayed horse, nobody believed this would work. At last a god who was known as "Treasure-thoughts" came up with an idea.

Hundreds of the gods set to work at once. There was a simple Sukaki tree growing on a hillside outside the cave and they decorated its branches with fabulous jewels, brightly colored ribbons and tiny mirrors. Then they began to sing, to dance, and to play musical instruments usually only brought out for the most important religious celebrations.

Hearing the noise, Amaterasu rolled back the stone and poked her head out. The sight that greeted her eyes astonished her. There were no fewer than eight hundred gods dancing outside the cave. Some were dressed only in bamboo leaves; others had stripped off altogether, much to the delight of the remainder who were howling with laughter and stamping their feet.

"What's happening?" Amaterasu demanded.

One of the gods turned and smiled at her. "Oh hello, Amaterasu," he said. "We thought you'd locked yourself away forever."

"So why are you celebrating?"

"Because now we have a goddess who's even more beautiful than you. She's going to take over."

"More beautiful than me?' Amaterasu's eyes opened wide. "And where can I find this . . . goddess?"

"She's just over there."

Amaterasu took three steps out of the cave. And there, a short distance away, she saw her rival. The "goddess" was sparkling brilliantly, living flames of color erupting from a cataclysm of blinding white. Ribbons of color fluttered in the breeze around her. Amaterasu took another three steps forward.

The colors grew even more dazzling, even more divine.

What she did not realize was that she was seeing only her own reflection, captured by the mirrors and the jewels on the Sukaki tree. For as she left the cave, her own golden light was returning to the heavens, bringing with it her own warmth, color, and life. When she was nine steps away, the god of Force suddenly leaped down and rolled the boulder back into place, tying it down so that the entrance was sealed. Then Amaterasu realized that she had been tricked.

But she was more angry with herself for being jealous of her own reflection than she was with the other gods for their cunning. And so she agreed to return to her place in the heavens. And that was the end of the first eclipse.

Glaucus and Scylla

Greek

There was, at a place called Anthedon, opposite Euboea, a secluded beach where the white sand formed a perfect crescent between the meadows and the sea. Although the fishermen who inhabited that part of the country sailed their ships up and down the coast, none had ever stepped on to that beach. For even from a distance they could feel that there was something strange about it . . . something not right.

It was nothing you could pin down. Perhaps the breeze was a little too still, the colors a little too intense. Perhaps the waves that broke against the sand seemed to pull back a little too quickly. It was certainly true that the animals, who can sense things no man ever can, avoided the place. No cattle or sheep grazed in the meadows. Even the bees passed over the flowers. At the end of the day, there was nothing you could put your finger on. But enchantment has its own peculiar smell and the beach at Anthedon stank of it.

But one evening, a fisherman returning home anchored his boat and came ashore to count the fish he had taken in his nets that day. His name was Glaucus, a young, cheerful man who feared nothing. He was in a good mood. It had been a hard day's work but, laying his fish in the sand, he could see that it was an excellent catch. Half a dozen snappers, twice as many mullet, and a prime swordfish lay stretched out in front of him.

A movement caught his eye. Was it his imagination or had the tail of the swordfish twitched? He blinked, then shook his head. The fish had been out of the water for an hour. It was impossible. It . . .

It twitched again. Then a couple of mullet flipped over. He looked more closely at his catch. All the fish had miraculously returned to life. Even as he sat there, with a reed that he had plucked from the beach clasped between his teeth, the fish began to wriggle back to the sea. He was too surprised to stop them. Often he had been told that Anthedon was enchanted. Now that he saw it with his own eyes he was more astonished than afraid. Only when the last fish had disappeared into the sea and he realized that he had lost his entire catch did he grit his teeth in vexation, breaking the reed.

Sap squirted into his mouth. He felt it on his tongue, tasting of honey. Before he could stop himself, he had swallowed it.

"Great heavens . . . !" he muttered.

His heart began to beat faster and faster. It felt as if his clothes were squeezing him to death and with scrabbling fingers he tore them off and ran until he stood naked on a cliff above the sea. But now the sun, though low in the sky, beat down on him. He looked down at the water. How inviting it was! How he longed to lose himself in its cool embrace. Despite his discomfort, he couldn't help laughing.

"Goodbye, world!" he cried. "You and I must part company."

Then he dived into the water, leaving his boat and his clothes to tell their own story.

Glaucus did not drown. As he sank farther and farther away from the air and the sun, he found (and it was a very agreeable surprise) that he could breathe. And, strangely, he felt at one with the element. It was like flying. He wasn't exactly wet as he would never again be exactly dry. The surface of the ocean was his sky, the sea-bed his land and he somersaulted between them, silent bubbles of laughter erupting from his mouth. He felt like a different man.

And a different man was just what he was. For the sap had transformed him in more ways than one. His beard, once light brown, was now a rusty green. His hair had more than doubled in length, flowing over shoulders that were suddenly much broader than they had ever been on land. His arms were dark blue. More peculiar than all of these metamorphoses put together, his legs had somehow become fused as one, becoming a fish's tail just around where the hips should have been. But a fish's tail was certainly a great deal more useful than two ungainly feet—as Glaucus soon found out. The merest flick could propel him at speed along the seabed and by twisting it he could dodge the coral and zigzag through the dunes.

So began his life under the sea. In the weeks that followed, he was introduced to the sea gods Oceanus and Tethys who welcomed him to their world. He rode on the backs of dolphins, reveling in their laughter as they raced across the surface of the sea. He discovered caves lit by phosphorescent stone where fish more beautiful than he had ever seen hid from the nets of the fishermen. He met the Oceanids, the three thousand nymphs of the oceans, and joined in their feasting. And he fell in love with Scylla.

Scylla was a Nereid, one of the nymphs

of the sea who come to the aid of sailors in distress. She was the loveliest creature he had ever seen either in the water or on land. He came upon her in a sunlit grotto where she was sitting on a rock, combing her long, fair hair. Although her shape was that of a human, she was no larger than a young girl. Her eyes were of a color caught somewhere between hazel and green. Her lips were full, her whole body lithe and graceful.

Glaucus swam toward her, then lay where the water was at its most shallow, propping himself against a rock. She saw him. He smiled. She screamed and dropped her comb.

"What . . . monster are you?"she cried.

"Monster?' Glaucus scratched his head indignantly. "I'm no monster, lady. My name is Glaucus. Don't let these blue arms of mine and all the rest of it put you off. Once I was a mortal . . . a fisherman (although in the circumstances, I tend not to mention it). Now I'm a sort of . . . mer-man, and the sea is my

home. The gods themselves have made me welcome—and may the gods bless them for it. Now, here's the thing, I couldn't help noticing you sitting here, and, well . . . I was wondering, you see, if . . .' Glaucus had gone very red but even as he spoke, Scylla had turned her back on him and run off into the forest. Then for the first time in a long time Glaucus was sad. He could not understand why Scylla should have rejected him so cruelly, even if his advances had been somewhat inept. What he did not know was that Scylla, rejoicing rather too much in her own beauty, rejected everybody. She had not yet found a man good enough for her in her own eyes and she did not care how she let her admirers know it.

But Glaucus was not to be deterred so easily. He had seen her only once but he knew that he could never forget her nor rest until she had accepted him. Now he turned and swam to the island of Aeaea. For he had heard tell of a powerful sorceress called Circe who lived there. And he needed her help.

This was the same Circe whom Odysseus would one day encounter on his wanderings after the Trojan War. The daughter of the sun god, Helios, she was a proud and mysterious goddess, skilled in every type of magic, but never to be trusted. She lived in a palace in the middle of a thick forest of oak trees where wolves and lions prowled—and not all of them had begun their lives as animals. For Circe delighted in feeding her guests potions that might turn them into a wolf or a lion . . . or something worse.

Glaucus came to her as she sat on the shore of her island, her eyes on the horizon, dreaming of secret things.

"Great Circe!" he cried. "I am only a humble man . . . well not exactly a man, as you can see, but humble all the same. I come to you for help. I know you're busy! But it won't take long . . . that is, if you agree to help."

Then Circe smiled. For Glaucus's looks pleased her as did his rough and awkward manner. "Speak on, little sea creature," she said. "What can I do for you?"

"Well, it's like this, your majesty. I'm in love with a Nereid, but the thing is, she isn't exactly crazy about me. Now, what I was hoping was that you could fix me up with some sort of potion . . . you know . . . magic herbs or something . . ."

"You want me to cure you of your love?" Circe interrupted.

"No! No! That's the last thing I want. No! It's for her. I want her to fall in love with me."

Circe looked at Glaucus thoughtfully.

"If, as you say, this Nereid has rejected you," she said, "then perhaps you should forget her. Would it not be more sensible to search for a woman who loves you as much as you might learn to love her? Someone like myself, for example. I may be a goddess, but I live alone on this island.

There is much I could offer you if you were to—"

"Oh no!" Glaucus burst in. "Begging your pardon, your highness, but that wouldn't be right at all. I mean . . . no offense. But seriously . . . !"

"You should forget this Nereid of yours," Circe snapped angrily.

"I can't!" Glaucus replied. "Leaves will grow in the sea and seaweed on the mountain tops before my feelings for Scylla change."

"Very well!" Circe said and if Glaucus had been looking more carefully, he would have seen two flames suddenly smolder in her eyes. "I will prepare you a potion that will change your Scylla . . ."

"You will?" Glaucus exclaimed in delight.

"Oh yes. It will change her. Wait for me here."

And with these enigmatic words, Circe swept away, disappearing into the darkness of the forest.

She returned an hour later, carrying a

small leather bag.

"Take the contents of this pouch," she said, "and sprinkle them in the water where your Scylla likes to swim. Inside there are certain roots over which I have chanted magic spells. Sprinkle them in the water and leave the place at once. I think the results will impress you."

"Thank you! Thank you!" Glaucus took the bag. "I will never forget you."

"No," Circe said. "You will never forget me."

Now every day Scylla liked to swim in a pool at Rhegium which lies near the steep rocks of Zancle. When the sun was at its hottest, she would dive into the crystal waters of the pool, then stretch herself out on the beach to dry. Glaucus found this out and one day, before she arrived, emptied the contents of the leather pouch on the surface. The roots that Circe had prepared were an ugly black and as they struck the water they hissed angrily. But not for a minute did he believe that they would do anything but win his love over to him.

Scylla arrived a short time later. As usual, she plunged into the pool, unaware that it had been polluted. She swam slowly but steadily, enjoying the cool of the water beneath the heat of the sun. Then, still dripping, she lay down on the beach and fell asleep.

She was awoken by a low growling. She half opened her eyes, then gasped in terror. A ferocious dog was sitting at her feet. There was another growl and she opened her eyes completely. Now she saw that there were no fewer than six of the monsters. She was surrounded by them. And these were no ordinary dogs. Their eyes bulged out of skulls that sat awkwardly on bony necks. Their skin was pitch black and hairless. Their teeth were sharklike.

Shuddering, terrified, she moved her arms an inch at a time, reaching for the sand behind her. If she could just pull herself clear

without disturbing them . . . She hooked her hand into the sand and dragged herself backward. As one, the six dogs followed her. Her heart was beating so painfully that she thought it would burst, but again she tried to ease herself away. She moved another six inches. The dogs moved another six inches. Then her nerve broke. She stood up and tried to run.

And then she realized with horror what had happened to her.

She could not run from the dogs. She could never run from the dogs. For the six animals were part of her, growing out of her.

She was standing on twelve legs. The horrible heads were sprouting out of her waist. With a ghastly scream, she scuttled back from the edge of the sea, moving like some grotesque spider. But the dogs bayed with delight. And far away, on the island of Aeaea, Circe laughed too.

Scylla remained where she was and ever

after sailors went in fear of her for she had no control over the six dogs which would tear travellers limb from limb and then slowly suck the pieces down.

And what of Glaucus?

"Leaves will grow in the sea and seaweed on the mountain tops before my feelings for Scylla change," he had said. But of course, leaves do grow in the sea and, as there are many underwater mountains, seaweed can be said to grow on mountain tops. Gradually his memory of Scylla and the rejection he had suffered faded. Then his old cheerfulness returned and he swam away to seek his fortune in the great expanse of the world's oceans.

But he never again went anywhere near the island of Aeaea.

The Spinning Contest

Greek

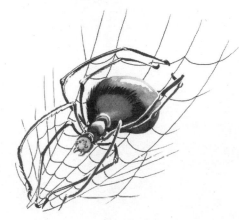

The Spinning Contest

In ancient Greece, it was always considered a wise move to thank the gods for a particular skill or talent that you happened to possess. If you really admired someone, you might go so far as to compare him to the gods. "He sings almost like Apollo," you might say— and you would be careful not to forget the "almost." But were you to claim that you did something as well as or even better than the gods . . . well, that could be very dangerous. In fact it could be lethal.

This is the story of just such a person, a girl by the name of Arachne. She was a young woman of Maeonia. Her family was poor and she had been born in a tiny cottage in the somewhat decrepit village of Hypaepa. Hypaepa was such a wretched place that the only people who visited invariably turned out to have lost their way and those who lived in it would really have preferred not to. Hypaepa didn't have a town green. It had a town moldy brown. Although it seldom rained, the main street was always full of puddles and the whole place smelled of fish.

Despite this inauspicious beginning, Arachne soon became famous throughout the country on account of her extraordinary skill at weaving. Then people did start coming to the village, simply to admire her work—and it wasn't only the finished product that made it worth the journey. To watch her weave, her fingers dancing over the pattern, was a pleasure in itself. There was an extraordinary elegance in the way she wound

66

yarn. To see her draw a single soft thread out of a great ball of fluff was like watching a conjuror. Whether she was twirling the spindle with a single flick of her thumb or embroidering the finished material, nobody could take their eyes off her.

You may think that this is all a little exaggerated, but watch any craftsman at work and you will see for yourself. A potter "growing" a vase between his fingers, a glassblower forming crystal bubbles over the flames, a carpenter stroking virgin wood with his chisel . . . there is a type of magic in craftsmanship and Arachne had plenty of it.

Unfortunately, she was somewhat less well endowed with the virtues of modesty, humility, and generosity. It is often the way that people who are particularly good at something are a little short on human kindness. Arachne had none at all. She was rude to her mother, quick-tempered with her servants, and generally difficult and unfriendly. But it was her arrogance that eventually undid her.

"I am so unbelievably, unusually, and extraordinarily talented," she remarked one day to her mother.

"Yes, dear," her mother said, stifling a yawn. She had heard it all before.

"Even the gods must envy me," she continued.

"Well, dear, I'm not so sure . . ."

"No god can weave as I can. Not even Athene. Compared to me, the so-called goddess of wisdom is just a clodhopper, a fat-fingered fumbler. I bet she's jealous of me. Everybody's jealous of me. But then I'd be jealous of me if I wasn't me. Because I'm so extravagantly talented."

Now this was a doubly foolish thing to say. For Athene was the goddess who had taught Arachne her skill in the first place. And secondly, she tended to react rather severely to insults such as these. In her twin role as goddess of war, she had once crushed one of her enemies to death using the entire island of Sicily. Her curses had caused one man to be flayed alive and another—the prophet Tiresias—to go blind. Athene was a kind and caring friend. But she was a terrible enemy.

But Arachne went on regardless.

"I bet Athene would never compete against me," she said. "She'd be too afraid of losing, especially against a supposed mortal. But then, perhaps there is a little goddess in me. What do you think? Don't you think I'm just a teeny-weeny bit divine?"

These words were no sooner out of her mouth than an old woman, who had somehow got into the room without anyone hearing her, stepped forward, supporting herself on a gnarled walking stick. She really was very old. Her hair was all white, her skin hanging in bags, and her eyes dim and blistered.

"Ugh!" Arachne exclaimed. "Who are you, old crone?"

"You shouldn't mock old age," the woman said. "For with it comes experience. Listen now to the voice of experience, Arachne. It is all very well to consider yourself the best mortal spinner. Perhaps you are. But you are wrong to compare yourself to the goddess Athene and should ask her pardon."

"Why should I?"

"Because she will forgive you if you ask. If you do not, who can say what she will do?"

Arachne scowled. She had been weaving when she was interrupted, but now she stopped, got up, and roughly pushed the old woman against the wall.

"You know what your problem is?" she said. "You're old. You're senile. Your brains have gone. You're like my mother. Don't you have daughters of your own to go and nag? Because don't imagine for a single minute that I care what you say. If Athene was so clever, she'd have come here herself. And even then I wouldn't apologize. I'd weave— and I can tell you, I'd show her a thing or two."

"Very well," the old woman said. "Now is your opportunity."

And suddenly she raised her arm, there was a burst of light and in an instant she was transformed. Gone were the old clothes, the walking stick, the wrinkles. In their place stood a tall, armored woman carrying a spear in one hand and a shield in the other. A helmet with five spikes surmounted her head and sheer power seemed to radiate around her.

"You have challenged me," Athene said,

for of course it was the goddess herself. "And I have come. Soon you may regret it."

When the transformation had taken place, many of the women in the room had fled, screaming with fear. But Arachne just smiled.

"I don't regret anything!" And so, while her mother watched, tight-lipped and pale, two looms were set up on opposite sides of the room. The goddess sat at one, the mortal at the other, back-to-back so that neither could see what the other was doing.

"Speed must count as well as technique," Athene said. "We will stop at sunset. Then we can compare what we have done."

"I'm ready when you are," Arachne said.
"Then we will start."

It was the strangest race that was ever run.
First the contestants stretched the threads
on their looms. They tied their frames to the
crossbeams, separated
the warp with their
heddles, reached
for their shuttles
to weave the
crossthreads . . .
in this way an
expert might
have described
it. But to the
onlookers,
unskilled in the

art of weaving, it was as if the two figures
were playing incredibly complicated,
multistringed instruments without actually
managing to make a single sound. For they
worked in silence, their fingers racing back
and forth across the frames, plucking and

pulling, dipping in and
out of the threads,
pulling, separating,
weaving . . .

And gradually two
pictures began to
form. First there
would be one color.
Then another. Then
a line of gold. A
shape. A hand . . .
then an arm. The hands continue their mad
pattern and a man springs to life, posing
against a background of Tyrian copper. A
man? No. The threads have been beaten back
by the comb and he has metamorphosed.
Below the waist he is a horse. Of course!

A centaur . . .

This is what the two contestants wove
that day:

Arachne wove a tapestry called "The Loves
of the Gods." It depicted Zeus no less than
three times but always in different guises:

as a bull, seducing Europa, as a swan in the arms of Leda, and as a shower of gold coins, tumbling into the lap of Danae. But Zeus was not the only god whose wickedness she portrayed. There was Poseidon as a bull, as a ram, and as a river—always as an adulterer. There was Apollo, disguised as a humble shepherd to deceive the simple country girl, Isse. And there was even the drunken god of wine, Bacchus, who had turned himself into a bunch of grapes in order to hang at the lips of the woman he loved. The tapestry was formed out of dozens of radiant colors. It was gaily decorated with a framework of flowers and ivy. But still it showed the gods at their most ignoble.

The theme of Athene's tapestry was very different for it was as flattering as Arachne's was irreverent. Here again was Zeus, but this time he was revealed in his full glory as king of Olympus, a thunderbolt in his hand and an eagle perched behind his throne. Poseidon stood with his trident, striking a

rock to release a
sparkling waterfall.
Athene herself appeared
in her own tapestry,
creating a mighty olive
tree simply by touching
the ground with her spear.
The tapestry was called
"The Power of the Gods."
But in each of the four corners
of her work, the goddess added
different scenes: scenes that would
have warned Arachne of her terrible
danger had she only been able to see it. For
they showed punishments that the gods
had inflicted on mortals unwise enough to

fall into their disfavor. There was Rhodope, changed into an icy mountain. Antigone and the queen of the pygmies both turned into birds. And Cinyras shedding bitter tears on the limbs of his dead daughters. Athene finished her work by embroidering the edges with olives: the symbols of peace.

The sun set and the contest ended. At last the two opponents stopped and turned around to face each other. Arachne's back was stiff and her fingers were sore and bleeding, but Athene was as fresh as when she had started.

"Now let us compare our work," Athene said.

Coldly, she ran her eye over "The Loves of the Gods."

"Hardly the way a mortal should represent the Olympians," she remarked. "But . . ." She pursed her lips. "The work is perfect."

"Of course it is," Arachne said smugly.

"It is. It's . . ."

"It's better than yours."

Then the goddess of wisdom and of war became angry because, astonished and disgusted though she was, she could not deny that Arachne was right. The mortal woman had beaten her at her own craft. Seeing Athene so indignant, Arachne broke into laughter, the shrill sound echoing around the room. But her mother trembled, seeing the blood run from Athene's face.

"Better than yours! Better than yours!" Arachne shouted.

"Enough!" the goddess cried.

Raising her shuttle, she struck Arachne

hard on the forehead, then again and again and again. Arachne screamed and fell to the floor. But the goddess had not finished yet. Forming a noose out of thread, she slipped it around Arachne's neck and while the wretched girl gurgled and grunted, drew it tight, pulling her off her feet so that she hung beneath the rafters.

It was then, seeing her daughter slowly strangle, that Arachne's mother threw herself forward, kneeling at the feet of the goddess.

"Great Athene!" she cried. "Forgive my little girl. She didn't know what she was doing. She doesn't mean to offend. It's just . . . well, she's a nasty piece of work . . . I admit it. But you can't kill her. I beg you . . . !"

Then Athene's heart softened. Regarding her foolish opponent who was now bright red, swaying like a pendulum in the air some six feet above the ground, she sprinkled her with a handful of herbs which had been prepared by the witch, Hecate.

"I will spare your life, wretch!" she said. "But this is how you must remain for all eternity. And this is how all your daughters shall be. Such is the punishment for your insolence and vanity."

The moment the poisoned herbs touched Arachne, all her hair fell out, immediately followed by her nose and ears. While her mother fainted dead away, Arachne's head shrank like a punctured balloon until it was no bigger than a pea. At the same time, her body folded in on itself, trapping her legs and arms, which disappeared

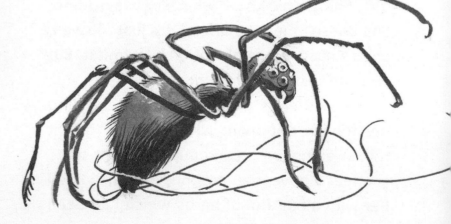

completely. Her fingers, which had scuttled so quickly across the threads, became stuck to her sides to serve her as legs. But they were thinner now, and hairy too.

And just as Athene had ordained, that was how Arachne remained. She still hung above the ground. And she still wove beautifully—although in not quite the same way.

For Arachne had been turned into a spider.

The Story of
the Panpipes

Greek

The Story of the Panpipes

Zeus, the king of the Greek gods, argued frequently with his wife, Hera. Many of these arguments were about young women, of whom Zeus was particularly fond. Unfortunately, it was often these young women who came off the worst from the arguments. Take the case of Io, for example. No sooner had Zeus fallen in love with her than he was forced to change her into a white heifer (a young cow) to keep her out of Hera's sight. But then Hera discovered the trick, captured Io and locked her up in a gloomy cave where she was guarded by a monster called Argus. Argus was well suited to the task because he had no less than one hundred eyes. No matter how long or how heavily he slept, at least two of these eyes would always remain open—so poor Io could never escape.

Eventually Zeus decided that Io had suffered enough and sent Hermes, the messenger of the gods, to kill Argus and rescue her. But Hermes had a problem.

There was no angle from which he could sneak up on Argus without being spotted, no way that he could take him by surprise. So instead he thought up a plan. He walked up to the cave boldly playing a set of panpipes and the sound of his music delighted Argus so much that the monster became friendly.

"Tell me, stranger," he growled (even when he was being friendly he still growled, so you can imagine what he was like when he was angry), "what is the instrument that you play so skillfully?"

"Why, sir," Hermes replied. "This is a set of panpipes."

"Panpipes?" Argus repeated. "What a strange name! Would I be right in thinking they have something to do with frying pans?"

"Not exactly," Hermes said, wondering why so many monsters were so very stupid. "As a matter of fact, they're named after my son."

"Your son? Clever boy! Tell me about him."

"With pleasure, sir."

Hermes sat down on the grass in front of the cave, stretching out his winged feet and laying his sword down beside him. It was a warm and sunny day and already Argus was feeling drowsy. No less than fifteen of his hundred eyes had closed. Eighty five to go, Hermes thought to himself. Then, with a smile, he began the story of the panpipes.

And this is how it went.

"Pan was the god of shepherds and of herds. He lived on the slopes of Mount Maenalus where the Arcadian shepherds came to worship him. For he was also the god of fertility and of growth. When you prayed to Pan, you knew that your flock was sure to increase.

"He was a strange fellow to look at. He was shaped like a man only as far down as the waist. Beneath that he was shaped like a goat with hairy legs, a tail, and hooves. He also had goat's ears although he partly concealed these under a wreath of pine leaves. Whatever his appearance, though, you couldn't help liking him. He was always laughing and singing and dancing. He was very partial to wine and frequently drank too much. Pan really was the merriest of gods. Only in the afternoon, when the sun was at its hottest, did he like to find a lonely and sheltered place where he could sleep in peace. To have woken him up at that time would have been a great mistake for his voice was so loud that it could turn a man's hair white and if he was in a really bad mood he would send you nightmares that would keep you awake for weeks."

Argus was not enjoying the story very much. It had begun promisingly, but there had been altogether too much description. If only the stranger would use fewer adjectives, he thought, I might enjoy it a little more. As it was, another twenty seven of his eyes closed in sleep.

"Pan was also a very lusty god. Nothing pleased him more than to chase girls across the fields until they were too exhausted to run any more. The girls, for their part, would scream when they saw him coming but secretly they were rather flattered by his attentions and made sure that they didn't run too fast.

"There was, however, one exception. Her name was Syrinx and she was a nymph, the most beautiful nymph Pan had ever seen. She had long, fair hair, pale skin, deep brown eyes, and a wonderfully slender body. The color in her cheeks was that of the sun on a spring morning."

Why doesn't he get to the point, Argus thought to himself. Another twenty four eyes closed. That made sixty six in all.

"Now Syrinx was a huntress and a worshipper of Artemis. Artemis was, as you may know, the goddess of the hunt and the moon and all nature. She was by nature strict and did not encourage casual affairs between young men and women. Syrinx worshipped Artemis so much that she even looked like her. Indeed she had often been mistaken for her when wearing her hunting dress and running barefoot through the woods. The only obvious difference between them was that Syrinx carried a bow made of horn whereas that of Artemis was made of gold. Anyway, having spent her life avoiding the company of men, you can imagine how Syrinx felt when she found herself pursued by a grinning half-man, half-goat.

"She screamed and ran. How she ran! She didn't stop for six hours. How many animals had run from her in just the same way as she now ran from Pan, crashing through the undergrowth, sobbing with each breath?

"Pan wouldn't give up. All his other conquests were forgotten as he raced after the nymph. She was lovely. She was enchanting.

The Story of the Panpipes

"She was fast! He thought that he would never catch her, but then he saw her slow down and stumble to a halt. A wide river ran through the forest—the River Ladon—and she had reached its edge. She could go no further. Pan laughed with excitement. He had her! The river was flowing too fast for her to be able to swim across. There was nowhere else to run. She was his!"

But Argus didn't care. Seventeen more eyes closed. Like so many monsters, he just didn't have the time for stories . . .

"Syrinx, finding herself trapped, raised her arms and called out to the nymphs who inhabited the waters of the river to protect her. And her sisters heard her. Pan rushed forward, but he was too late. Just when he thought he had her in his arms, he found that she was gone and all that remained was a handful of marsh reeds.

"He stood there beside the river, sighing to himself. But then, as he turned to leave, the wind blew through the reeds making a strange, sad sound—almost like music. Hearing it, the smile returned to Pan's face and he turned back.

"'Syrinx!' he exclaimed. 'You may have escaped me, but together we can still make music.'

"And so saying, he leaned down and cut reeds of different lengths and fastened them together with wax. This was how the first panpipe was made. And panpipes are still played to this very day."

Argus was no longer listening. His last two eyes had closed. All one hundred of them were shut. It was what Hermes had been waiting for. Gently, he lifted his sword, then brought it whistling through the air. The monster's head parted company with his shoulders and his body rolled away down the hill. Then Hermes went into the cave and although Io's troubles were far from over, at least she was delivered from her prison.

Hera, when she saw what had happened

to her servant, took his eyes and used them to decorate the feathers of her favorite bird. The next time you see a peacock spread its tail, look closely. You will have seen the hundred eyes of Argus.

The Monkey Who Would Be King

Chinese

The Monkey Who Would Be King

The Chinese tell many stories about a monkey whose full name was Sun Hou-tzu and who was hatched from an egg at the top of a mountain on the eastern side of the ocean. Although he was only a monkey, a wizard taught Sun all the secrets of the art of magic and soon he was able to change into seventy two different forms and could jump thirty six thousand miles with a single bound.

Sun was not a villain to begin with. It was he who organized all the world's monkeys into a single great army. By putting them all on the same side, he made sure that there was nobody for them to fight against which is why the monkeys have always been at peace. Unfortunately, this accomplishment went to his head and he began to get rather too big for his boots.

Stealing a magic sword from the Dragon King of the Eastern Sea, he made a nuisance of himself in all kinds of different ways. He got drunk at a banquet and woke up in Hell where he promptly killed the two devils who guarded him and tore his name out of the Book of the Dead. This meant that he could never die. He was sent up to Heaven where he looked after the stables, but when he got bored with that, he broke down one of Heaven's walls and escaped back to Earth.

Soon all the gods and goddesses were furious with him. The entire army of Heaven set out after him and although he fought valiantly, changing into all seventy two of his different shapes, he was caught and sentenced to death. But because he couldn't die, it was decided instead to melt him down in the furnace of a famous wizard called Laozi.

Laozi made his furnace white hot and dropped the monkey inside, slamming the lid. Sun remained there for forty nine days, but then, when nobody was looking, he opened the lid and sprang out. By that time he was white hot with anger. Snatching up his magic sword, he announced himself the King of

Heaven and threatened to kill everyone who lived there.

Now the August Personage of Jade, who was the proper ruler of Heaven, was at his wits' end. He could not kill the monkey and it seemed he could not keep him a prisoner. So in despair he sent for the one being who was more powerful than him—more powerful, in fact, than anyone or anything in the universe. The Buddha.

And so the Buddha came and asked the monkey what all the fuss was about.

"I want to be King of Heaven," the monkey told him.

"Do you think you are ready for such a position?" the Buddha asked, with a gentle sigh.

"Of course I am," the monkey snapped. "I'm ready for anything. Did you know, for example, that I can change myself into seventy two different shapes? And that I can jump thirty six thousand miles with one bound? I bet you can't jump that far."

102

"You think yourself more powerful than me?" the Buddha asked.

"I most certainly do."

"Let us see, then, my little friend. Show me how far you can jump. But to prove that you really go as far as you say, write your name on the ground when you get there."

So the monkey took a deep breath, crouched down and with all his strength leaped into the air. It was a fantastic jump. He soared up into the sky, broke through the clouds and continued into outer space, past the planets, right out of the solar system and beyond the stars. At last he landed in the middle of a great desert where two huge trenches met in the ground in front of him. Nothing grew for thousands of miles in any direction, but he could see that the ground was laced with a network of lines, making intricate patterns as they crossed over one another. Sun Hou-tzu had no idea where he was, but he was terrifically pleased with himself. He signed his name on the ground

with a great flourish and jumped all the way back again.

"Not bad," the Buddha said. "But I'm sure you can do even better than that. Why not try again? And this time put all of your strength into it."

"Okay," Sun said.

He puffed himself up so much that he looked more like a frog than a monkey. Then he scrunched himself into a ball and finally catapulted himself off the ground with legs like rockets. This time he shot through the universe so quickly that he was just a blur. Not only did he break out of the solar system, but he passed the five red pillars which mark the boundary of the created world. At last he landed, this time on the edge of a perfectly circular cliff. A white precipice jutted out just below the ground on which he stood and beneath that all was darkness. The height almost made him dizzy, but he still signed his name as he had been told before jumping all the way back.

"There you are!" he said to the Buddha, unable to stop himself sneering. "I have proved that I am more powerful even than you. Could you have jumped that far? Of course not! Only the monkey could do it!"

"Wretched creature!" the Buddha cried, getting angry for the first time. He stretched out his hand. "See here the full extent of your vanity. You have signed your name twice on my right hand. The first time you landed on my palm, between my life line and my line of destiny. The second time you reached as far as the tip of my index finger and stood above my nail. Look where you have made your mark. It is the evidence of your own limitations!"

Now the monkey was afraid and began to tremble. He opened his mouth to speak, but it was too late for words.

The Buddha seized the wretched creature and shut him up in a magic mountain. And there he remained until the day that he forgot his ambitions and realized that although a

monkey can rule the world, only the Buddha
is fit to rule the kingdom of Heaven.

You've really changed . . .

The Greek myths are full of unfortunate transformations. Here are six of the worst

Io: from nymph to heifer . . .

sixth place

It was never good news when the king of the gods fell in love with you. Io was a nymph and a priestess until she caught the eye of Zeus. He turned her into a heifer (a young cow) to hide her from his jealous wife, Hera.

And if that wasn't bad enough, Hera discovered the truth and sent a swarm of stinging flies to chase Io across the world. Some people say she was eventually stung to death. Not a happy tale.

Lycaon: from king to wolf . . .

fifth place

If you've been reading these stories you should know that it was never wise to play tricks on the gods. Lycaon was a king of Arcadia, who fed his own son to Zeus, chopped up, to see if he would know what he was eating.

As a punishment, Zeus turned Lycaon into a wolf. He also killed all fifty of Lycaon's sons except for the one he had eaten. He returned that one to life. I'm not completely sure what the point of this story is meant to be.

Arachne: from weaver to spider . . .

fourth place

Arachne has turned up quite a few times in these stories. She was a famous weaver who made the mistake of challenging Athene (goddess of wisdom) to a duel to prove that her skills were greater.

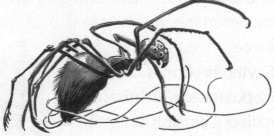

She won the competition but was turned into a spider as a punishment. Arachne is actually the Greek word for spider, and arachnophobia, an English word derived from the Greek, means "fear of spiders."

Scylla: from Egyptian girl to monster . . .

third place

As monsters go, you couldn't get much worse than Scylla. She had six dogs' heads, each one with four eyes and three rows of razor-sharp teeth. She also had twelve legs which were like tentacles, and the tail of a cat. She was turned into this monster by the famous sorceress, Circe.

Scylla lived in a cave opposite a whirlpool called Charybdis, in the Strait of Messina. Even today, if someone says you are between Scylla and Charybdis it means that, all in all, you don't have much of a choice.

Medusa: from beauty queen to snake-haired ogre

second place

I've told the story of Medusa in one of the other books of myths and legends. She was a renowned beauty, one of three sisters, until she slept with Poseidon (the sea god) in the temple of Athene. This was sacrilege and, as a result, Athene turned her into a gorgon, a hideous monster with snakes instead of hair.

She was so horrific that anyone who looked at her was turned instantly to stone. You might like to know that the word "petrified" actually means "turned to stone" and may find its origin here.

Actaeon: from hunter to stag to dog's dinner

first place

You'll find the story of Actaeon in this collection. Actaeon was a famous hunter who stumbled upon Artemis, the goddess of hunting, while she was bathing naked in the woods. Before he had time to apologize, she turned him into a stag.

He wins first place, not because of the transformation itself but because of what happened afterward. He was torn to pieces by his own hounds.

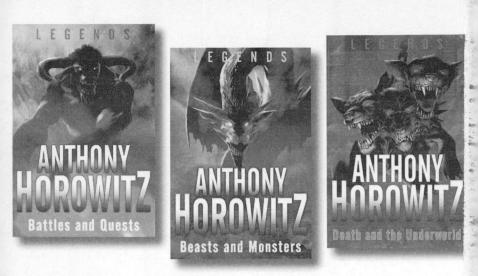

LEGENDS

ANTHONY HOROWITZ
Battles and Quests

LEGENDS

ANTHONY HOROWITZ
Beasts and Monsters

LEGENDS

ANTHONY HOROWITZ
Death and the Underworld

COLLECT THEM ALL!

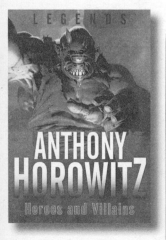

LEGENDS

ANTHONY HOROWITZ
Heroes and Villains

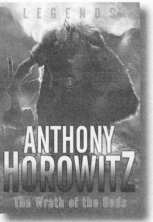

LEGENDS

ANTHONY HOROWITZ
The Wrath of the Gods

LEGENDS

ANTHONY HOROWITZ
Tricks and Transformations